WEDNESDAY WILSON

FIXES ALL YOUR PROBLEMS

To my kids, who lent their voices and experiences to help bring Wednesday to life, and to all the kids like them who believe they can create change. This is for you! — B.G.

Text © 2022 Bree Galbraith
Illustrations © 2022 Morgan Goble

Published in Canada and the U.S. by Kids Can Press Ltd.
25 Dockside Drive, Toronto, ON M5A 0B5

Kids Can Press is a Corus Entertainment Inc. company

www.kidscanpress.com

The artwork in this book was rendered digitally.
The text is set in Baskerville.

Edited by Katie Scott
Designed by Andrew Dupuis

Printed and bound in Shenzhen, China, in 10/2021 by C & C Offset

CM 22 0 9 8 7 6 5 4 3 2 1

Library and Archives Canada Cataloguing in Publication

Title: Wednesday Wilson fixes all your problems / written by Bree Galbraith ; illustrated by Morgan Goble.

Names: Galbraith, Bree, author. | Goble, Morgan, 1996– illustrator.

Identifiers: Canadiana 20210200022 | ISBN 9781525303289 (hardcover)

Classification: LCC PS8613.A4592 W39 2022 | DDC jC813/.6 — dc23

Kids Can Press gratefully acknowledges that the land on which our office is located is the traditional territory of many nations, including the Mississaugas of the Credit, the Anishnabeg, the Chippewa, the Haudenosaunee and the Wendat peoples, and is now home to many diverse First Nations, Inuit and Métis peoples.

We thank the Government of Ontario, through Ontario Creates; the Ontario Arts Council; the Canada Council for the Arts; and the Government of Canada for supporting our publishing activity.

Written by BREE GALBRAITH

Illustrated by MORGAN GOBLE

KIDS CAN PRESS

CONTENTS

*Skip to page 14 for the REAL start to the story.

CHAPTER 1
Worrywart

I sometimes worry that all the best businesses have already been started by other people. I have ideas that sound good in my head, but in real life they only seem to get me in trouble. Maybe I'm not cut out to be an entrepreneur after all, and I should become an environmentalist — that's what all the kids in my class want to be when they grow up.

Usually when I worry about giving up on my dream, it's because I'm already in a funk. My nonno used to say a funk is when you're in a bad mood and you let everything upset you, which only makes it worse. He also told me funks can be contagious.

WARNING! Only keep reading if you promise you won't get mad at me if my funk rubs off on you.

I'm glad you're still reading. Anyway, I don't think I caught my funk from anyone. It all started this morning when we had breakfast pizza from my mum's food truck, the Teresaria, for the eleventh day straight. If you don't know what breakfast pizza is, it's when your mom puts a fried egg on leftover pizza and says, "Breakfast is ready!" Have you ever told your parents you don't want to eat their food? In my house, it goes something like this:

Me: This tastes like it should be illegal.

Mom: It's good for you, and I'd like you to try it.

Me: I am not in the mood for *[insert gross food here]*.

Mom: This is not a restaurant, so this is what you're eating.

Me: *[Eats gross food but is not happy about it.]*

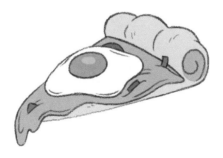

But this morning it went even worse because I refused to eat her eggy pizza, which was right around the time I realized I was in a funk and became a worrywart about my next business idea. My mom was so annoyed with me that she phoned my mum at work for backup. But it sounded like a bad time to call, because someone's dog had just run off with all her pepperoni! So Mum said she didn't have time to talk to me. And then my moms got in a fight.

My brother, Mister, hates it when our parents argue. He just sat there, still as a statue at the kitchen table, holding his breath as he listened.

Ever since Mom hung up the phone, Mister's been sitting here all gloomy. Remember how I said funks are contagious? Well, I think mine might have rubbed off on my mom, then on my mum and finally on Mister.

I try to get Mister's attention because it's almost time to leave for school, but he's ignoring me. So I take the jumbo marble I found in the fruit bowl and aim for his glass of orange juice.

CLINK! Direct hit! But then the unthinkable happens. The glass teeters and falls over. Orange juice streams onto the table, all over the breakfast pizza and all over Mister's homework.

"You ruined everything!" shouts Mister, holding up his family tree project, which is now dripping wet.

"Maybe now it's an orange tree?" I say, trying to lighten the mood. I bet you already know that didn't work.

"WEDNESDAY WILSON!" my mom yells. "Not another word! Eat your breakfast and go straight to school!"

She tosses me a cloth to mop up the mess and heads to her art studio without saying goodbye. I should have just eaten the breakfast pizza in the first place, because now everyone's upset with me and I still have to eat it anyway. Could this day get any wor—

THE REAL CHAPTER 1
Starting Over

Do you ever wish you could start a bad day over? I've decided my day actually begins the exact moment we leave our house and walk to school. Now I just need something to cheer me up, so I think of that dog with its belly full of pepperoni, because dogs always make things better. It makes me smile, and I can tell it's working!

If Mister's bad mood is my fault, then I have to help him out of his funk, too. It's the least I can do. I offer to carry Mister's family tree project because I guess you could say it's my fault that it's a soggy mess.

One of the paper branches breaks off, and I'm desperately trying to hide it from him so he doesn't get more upset. Fortunately, Mister hasn't noticed yet because he's trying to kick a lucky rainbow marble, like a tiny soccer ball, all the way to school.

Technically it's *my* lucky rainbow marble, but after the trouble I caused him this morning, I'm letting him play with it.

My nonno gave me the marble before he died, which is why it's special. He told me it's called an "onion skin" because it has so many colorful lines that look like an onion cut in half. Nonno said this marble reminded him of me, since it has so many beautiful layers and no two are alike. He told me there was a marble for every person out there.

MARBLE

ONION

Nonno collected marbles his whole life, and he used to give me one whenever we visited. When Nonno died last year, my nonna gave me his whole collection to look after because her new apartment doesn't have space. I'm not sure *we* even have space, since there are marbles all over our house! But I think my mum secretly likes having them around because they remind her of her dad and she really misses him.

"Hey, Wednesday?" Mister finally speaks.

"Yes?" I answer.

"You should sell plates with trapdoors that can hide gross breakfast."

"Good idea!" I tell him. Then I write it down on my clipboard, where I keep all my best business ideas. And we even come up with a few more.

BUSINESS IDEAS
GOOD ENOUGH TO EAT

- trapdoor plate to hide gross breakfast (could hide kale, too?)
- chocolate straw that turns regular milk into chocolate milk
- ice-cube tray shaped like letters so we can put words in our orange juice
- catapult fork that sends food scraps to your dog across the room
- cup that never spills, even if someone hits it with a marble

18

We might be onto something. I'll ask my best friend, Charlie, what he thinks of our ideas when I see him in class, since he's getting a ride today after staying with his dad for the weekend. When I look up at Mister to smile, he isn't smiling back because he has discovered his broken tree.

"My family tree is even more ruined!" Mister cries.

I try to think of something I can say to help. Then I remember what Nonna always tells us. "Worrying gives small things a big shadow," I tell him. "You can fix it when you get to school."

Mister doesn't look convinced. "Some things can't be fixed, Wednesday!" he exclaims.

Then he kicks the marble ahead of him and stomps after it. When we're finally on school grounds, he tries a bunch of times to get it over the curb in front of the main door. He finally rolls it onto the top of his shoe and flings it as high as he can. My prized rainbow marble flies through the air and over all the students hustling into school.

"That was your lucky marble!" says Mister, trying not to lose sight of it.

We watch as the marble bounces off Principal Webb's head and lands inches from her feet.

"Not so lucky anymore," I tell him.

CHAPTER 2
A Toilet Emergency

Principal Webb reaches down and picks up the marble, then looks around suspiciously at all the kids rushing past her. Mister and I pretend to look at my clipboard, then we run by her when she's not looking.

When I get to class, I'm surprised to see Charlie is already at his desk. He's usually late on the days his dad drives him to school. I don't have time to say hi because Ms. Gelson gets started right away.

"Buenos dias!" Ms. Gelson says to the class. Every month, she chooses a different language to say good morning, and this

month it's Spanish. "Everybody, grab your desk. It's time to meet your new neighbors!"

Ms. Gelson asks for a drumroll. She turns over a piece of paper on the easel at the front of the class to reveal the new seating arrangement. Randall is the only one who drums.

Please no Emmas. Please no Emmas. I take a deep breath and scan for my name on the new seating chart.

My new group has my friend Amina, Dustin (who always blames his farts on others) and … Emmet. Emmet is one of the Emmas, who have been mean to me and Charlie ever since kindergarten. But the meanest thing they ever did was steal my other best friend, Ruby, who now goes by Ruby Beautiful.

Looking around the class, I can tell no one is happy with the new arrangements.

One of the Emmas is fake crying because they have all been split up. And Charlie now has to sit next to Emma M., the meanest Emma of them all. At least Amina is in my new group, and I'm still next to our class lizard, Morten. I quickly push my desk even closer to Morten's terrarium and wait for Amina as she moves across the room.

"Hi, Wednesday," says Amina as she pushes her desk next to mine. She looks over at Dustin and whispers, "I hope he didn't have beans for breakfast."

I am about to laugh, when Ms. Gelson interrupts for an announcement.

"Congratulations!" she says to the class. "You broke the seating change record by two whole minutes. You know what that means …"

She reaches into her desk and pulls out a pink jelly bean. I think it's a watermelon one, and my mouth waters. Randall does another drumroll as Ms. Gelson walks over to the jar on the windowsill.

"Another jelly bean in the reward jar!" she says as she drops it in.

We're close to filling the jar, which equals a class party with jelly beans on the menu.

After we move our desks, Ms. Gelson explains the morning's writing assignment. "Today we begin our class project for Poetry Month. The theme this year at Harbor View Elementary is Poet-Tree. Each class is using poetry to explore how we're all connected, just like how trees are connected to the earth, the air and the creatures that live in them."

Ms. Gelson asks us to come up with questions to ask our desk mates. We need to find one thing we all have in common and then write a poem about it.

I brainstorm some questions on a blank page.

- ~~What do you want to be when you grow up?~~
- ~~What do you like most about dogs?~~
- ~~What did you eat for breakfast?~~
- If you had a thousand dollars to start a business, what would it be?

That's it! My question is not only fun but also useful for R&D.*

*R&D stands for "research and development." It's how a company figures out what products people actually want to buy. I heard about it on my favorite TV show, *Eagle Eye*. That's the one where people with an eye for business try to get millionaires to invest in their ideas.

I ask Amina my question first, because she's the smartest person in our class and probably has tons of great business ideas.

"I'd like to start a business that helps people, not just sell them something," she says.

Good idea! I write down her answer.

I ask Dustin next. He doesn't take anything seriously, so I doubt he'll be helpful. He thinks about it for a really long time. Or maybe he's trying to hold in a fart.

"I'd take the thousand dollars and run!" he finally says.

I'm about to tell him that's not an option, when I hear someone whispering my name. Am I hearing things?

I turn around to see Mister's friend Dakota peeking into our classroom. Emmet has noticed, too, because he has superhuman hearing when it comes to other people's business.

"What are you doing here?" Emmet whispers back.

Dakota doesn't answer. Instead, he waves me over. This makes Emmet try harder to get involved.

Ms. Gelson is busy helping Randall, so I take the opportunity while she's not watching to go see what Dakota wants. Emmet follows me.

"Dakota! Are you okay?" I ask him.

"Wednesday," Dakota says, completely out of breath, "I need your help. It's sort of an emergency."

"What kind of emergency?" asks Emmet. "Should I get Ms. Gelson?"

"No!" Dakota and I whisper at the same time.

"Then you better tell me what's going on," demands Emmet.

Dakota thinks about it for a second. "If you must know, it's a bathroom emergency."

Emmet scrunches up his face and looks down at Dakota's pants, like Dakota's peed them. "You're so immature," he says loudly on his way back to his desk. It's enough to get everyone's attention, including Ms. Gelson's.

Charlie has turned bright red with secondhand embarrassment. He's about to blurt out one of his facts, which always happens when he's stressed out.

"The average person uses the toilet twenty-five hundred times a year!" Charlie blurts out.

The whole class starts laughing uncontrollably. Dustin laughs so hard he almost falls off his chair.

"Wednesday," Ms. Gelson says as she makes her way to us, "what's this all about?"

Great. Just when I thought I'd turned this day around!

Dakota tugs at my sleeve and pulls me down to whisper in my ear. "It's Mister. He's sort of stuck in the toilet. We need to go. NOW."

CHAPTER 3
Down in the Dumps

My head is spinning searching for something to say to Ms. Gelson so I can leave class with Dakota.

"Mister needs my help with a … a … a bathroom thing," I blurt out.

In case you ever need them, the words *bathroom thing* are usually enough to stop people from asking questions.

Ms. Gelson agrees to let me go, as long as I take a buddy. I'm about to ask Charlie, when she says, "Emmet, you can go with Wednesday, since you were also up from your desk."

I don't have time to protest.

Emmet and Emma M. lock eyes and wink twice. Clearly it's their secret eye-shake for "spy on them and report back."

We leave the class and follow Dakota down the stairs two at a time.

"How stuck is he?" asks Emmet as we approach the boys' bathroom. "Will we need the custodian?"

"No." Dakota rolls his eyes. "His *butt* isn't stuck. He says he's never leaving the stall!"

I have to admit, this isn't as exciting as someone actually being stuck in a toilet. But it's a lot cleaner.

"Did he tell you why?" I ask.

"He freaked out about tomorrow's assembly," Dakota tells me. "Our class is reciting a poem about our family trees in front of the whole school."

I can hear Mister's muffled cries from inside, and I know what I need to do.

"Stay here and keep watch," I tell Emmet. Then Dakota and I go inside the boys' bathroom.

If you've never been in a boys' bathroom before, I have to warn you that you're in for a surprise. They have these things on the wall called urinals that are used for peeing standing up. There's only one stall, and Mister has locked himself inside.

"Mister?" I say as I knock on the bathroom stall. "I can help you fix the broken branch!"

"My tree may as well stay broken. Our family is going to split in half once our moms get a divorce!"

"Get a WHAT?" I say, panicked.

"You heard them fighting this morning," says Mister. "What if that means they're getting divorced? I'm already scared to stand up in front of the school tomorrow, and it's going to be even worse if I have to lie about our family being happy."

"Is that what you were so worried about on the way to school?" I ask. "First of all, our moms are not getting divorced. And second of all —"

But before I can continue, the bathroom door opens and Emmet walks in. Great.

"Mister?" says Emmet. "I heard what you said, and I know how you feel."

So he *was* spying on us!

Mister gulps and sniffles. "You do?" he asks.

"I was scared to do the family tree assignment when I was in kindergarten," Emmet replies. "I've never met my dad, so I was worried I'd fail if I couldn't fill in his side of the tree."

"You thought that?"

I never pictured Emmet worried about failing anything, since he and the rest of the Emmas always get good grades.

"Did you fail?" asks Mister, sniffing away the last of his tears.

I want to tell Mister that you can't fail anything in kindergarten, but I hold back. Emmet seems to be cheering him up, so I let him keep going.

"No way," Emmet tells him. "I had the coolest tree in the whole class and couldn't wait to show it off to the school!"

"But how?" asks Dakota.

"It was my mom's idea. She drew a big tree house on the empty side of the tree. She explained that it doesn't always matter how everyone is connected by the branches, and that we could fill the tree house with our chosen family, like friends and neighbors."

I've never seen this side of Emmet before, being so nice and helpful, so I'm pretty sure my mouth is hanging wide open. And come to think of it, Emmet's tree definitely was the coolest in our kindergarten class.

"Mister." I knock again. "Why don't you come out so we can make a plan like Emmet and his mom did?"

Mister unlocks the door and steps out of the stall. "I'm still worried about standing up in front of the whole school."

"You just need a worry stone," Emmet replies, "and you'll be fine!"

"I don't have a worry stone," Mister says. "I don't even know what that is!"

To tell you the truth, I don't know what a worry stone is either.

"It's a stone that helps you take your mind off your worries," Emmet tells Mister before I need to ask. "When you're upset about something, you focus on the stone in your hand instead of the bad stuff."

"I need a worry stone, Wednesday," Mister says, and I can tell he's getting upset again.

Think, Wednesday. THINK! "Mister, if you go back to class, I'll get you a worry stone by recess!" I blurt out.

Mister agrees, and we all leave the boys' bathroom together and head our separate ways.

"What do you think you're doing?" asks Emmet as he and I walk up the stairs.

"I'm going back to class," I tell him. "What are you doing?"

"That's not what I mean, Wednesday," Emmet replies, in the same know-it-all voice the Emmas always use. And just like that, he's back to his old self.

"Well, it's a half-truth," I tell him. "I'm also forming a business plan in my head."

"A worry stone is a real thing. You can't

just make it up like the rest of your business stuff," Emmet says.

I ignore him. Entrepreneurs like me don't have time to listen to people who don't believe in us. But you already know from earlier that Emmet doesn't like being ignored.

"If you don't tell me what your plan is, I might have to let Principal Webb know you were in the boys' bathroom …"

"You'd be doing me a favor," I say, "because the principal's office is exactly where I need to be."

CHAPTER 4
Dodging Questions

Emmet and I start running back to class, but then our class runs into us! They are being led by Mr. Yah, our gym teacher, who's always smiling, always moving and always wearing short shorts, even in the winter.

"There you are!" exclaims Mr. Yah with a big smile. "Ms. Gelson sent us to pick you up on the way to gym class. Jump on the dodgeball train!"

We head downstairs to the changing rooms and, after putting on our gym clothes, meet back in the gym. Mr. Yah divides us into two teams. Charlie and I are on the same team, but so is Emma M. On the other team are Amina, Emmet and Ruby. The other two Emmas are split up, so they do what they always do when this happens: act like it's the last time they'll see each other. Watching them act like this is one of the worst parts about dodgeball, but there are a lot of good parts, too.

Mr. Yah lines up all the balls in the middle of the gym and blows his whistle. I have several dodgeball tactics, and running first for the balls is one of them. But today I wait at the back of the gym with Charlie because I have to fill him in on the plan.

BEST PARTS ABOUT DODGEBALL

- I've been the last one standing seven times in a row.
- Charlie cheers for me from the sidelines.
- You can throw balls at people you don't like and not get in trouble.
- It's better than math class.

WORST PARTS ABOUT DODGEBALL

- It's not an Olympic sport, so I'll probably never make it to the Olympics for anything.
- Charlie always gets out first, so we hardly get to play together.
- The Emmas overreact about the ball stinging when they get hit.
- Ruby and I used to work together to win when we were on the same team. I miss that.

"I need to get to the principal's office," I explain to Charlie.

WHOOSH! A ball rushes toward me. I catch it midair, and Jackson is automatically out.

"On purpose?" asks Charlie. We both dodge the same ball, and Charlie hands it to me after it bounces off the wall behind us.

"Yes!" I use the ball to block another ball coming my way, which rebounds and

hits Althea, who's on the other team. "And I need to get there before recess."

For this to work, I have to break my winning streak.

I toss the ball across the line, and it hits the ground right beside Emmet's feet. Emmet picks it up and looks right at me.

"What are you waiting for? Get her out!" Emma M. demands, even though we're on the same team.

Emmet throws the ball at me. I have
tons of time to get out of the way, but
instead I bend down to fix my shoelace.
The ball hits me right on the forehead, and
I fall to the floor.

TWEEEEEEET! Mr. Yah blows his whistle. *TWEET! TWEET!*

Charlie and Amina run over to see if I'm okay.

"I think I need an ice pack," I say, clutching my head.

"OMG, Mr. Yah. Wednesday did this on purpose!" says Emma M. "She's trying to get Emmet in trouble!"

"No one is in trouble," Mr. Yah says, ignoring Emma M.'s protests. "Charlie, please go to the nurse's office with Wednesday."

"But she's not even hurt!" cries Emma M. She starts to speak again, when Emmet shushes her. He glances over at me and Charlie as I hobble out the door.

CHAPTER 5
Top Secret Mission

As we walk down the hall, I fill Charlie in on what happened in the boys' bathroom, right up to the point where going to the office was the next step in the plan.

"So what does Principal Webb have to do with this?" asks Charlie.

"You might not like my answer," I reply.

Charlie's not the greatest in nerve-racking situations, and I worry my answer will only make him more nervous.

"I need to help Mister, right?" I ask. I already know he won't disagree with that.

"Yes," says Charlie.

"And it's about time we started another business, right?"

"It would be fun," Charlie agrees.

"Well, Principal Webb has the solution to both problems. My lucky marble! It's in her office, and I need to get it back. The only tiny issue is that she can't know it's mine," I tell him.

We're walking up the stairs to the office, and Charlie stops mid-step. "Wednesday, why can't she know it's yours?"

"I didn't have much to do with it, but the marble accidentally hit her on the head this morning."

"Wednesday! This does NOT *sssound* good," he hisspers at me. (*Hisspering* is when you hiss and whisper at the same time. You can use the word, too, but just know that I'm going to trademark* it someday.)

"It's going to be okay, Charlie," I try to reassure him, "but you don't have to help me if you don't want to."

My mum told me business leaders have to convince people their ideas are worth

---

*A trademark is a word or logo that you own so that nobody can copy you. You can even trademark a sound or smell. I wonder if Dustin will trademark his farts one day.

taking risks for, but that pressuring people into taking risks will never work. They will just quit on you. And I never want Charlie to quit on me.

"I will always help you with business stuff," he says, "but I'm still not sure about sneaking into Principal Webb's office."

"I can do that part alone, but can you do one small thing? Can you stay here and make animal noises if Principal Webb comes?"

"Okay," Charlie agrees.

I walk into the office as normally as possible, which is hard to do when you're *trying* to act normal.

"Wednesday!" Mrs. Dawson, the school secretary, smiles when she sees me. "What can I help you with?"

"Mr. Yah sent me to get an ice pack," I tell her a bit too quickly. Then I remind myself to act normal. After all, I'm not lying. He *did* send me.

"Is someone hurt?" she asks. Clearly I do not look injured.

"Me!" I tell her. "I was hit in the head during dodgeball."

"Not too hard, I hope," Mrs. Dawson says as she heads to the nurse's room. "One ice pack, coming right up!"

"Nope, not too hard, and thank you!" I reply as I hurry into Principal Webb's office. I get right to work looking for my lucky marble, but I can't find it anywhere!

"Animal noises!" calls Charlie from the office door. "Animal noises! Animal noises!"

"I need more time, Charlie! Stall!" I whisper from Principal Webb's office. "And also, you were supposed to make actual animal noises."

"Sorry, I panicked!" says Charlie, and then he runs down the hall. I can hear him blurt out one of his facts to Principal Webb.

My stomach turns at the thought of opening one of her desk drawers. But as I walk around the desk, I see my marble in front of a framed picture of a young Principal Webb holding a tiny puppy! It's proof that everyone in the world has a dog but me. I snatch up the marble from the bowl and leave her office as fast as I can.

I rush to Mrs. Dawson's side and grab
the ice pack before she has a chance to look
up. "I feel better already!" I tell her as I
hold the ice pack to my head.

Charlie looks thankful to see me in the
hall, but Principal Webb seems confused.

"Some people take dodgeball too
seriously," I explain, and I lean on Charlie
as we walk back to gym class.

CHAPTER 6
Let the Magic Begin!

At recess, Charlie, Amina and I find Mister and Dakota at the kindergarten entrance. Emmet is there, too, and explains that he wanted to make sure he didn't hit me too hard during dodgeball. For the first time, I'm kind of glad to see Emmet because I can show him my worry-stone idea and prove to him how seriously I take my new ventures.

I show everyone the marble, but they aren't as excited as I expected. Even when I say, "Ta-da!"

"You got your marble back?" asks Mister.

"It's not just a marble! It's a Worry Marble! And it can help fix all your problems." I say that last part loudly.

A few of Mister's classmates hear me and start to gather around. Now's my chance to get people excited about my business idea. I hand Mister the marble, and he holds it up in the air, where it catches the light and shines like a magic crystal.

"My nonno taught me everything about marbles," I tell the crowd. "See the red inside this one? That's for courage. We have Worry Marbles in all different colors that can help with any problem."

More kids from different grades have joined us, and they're all staring at the marble in Mister's hand.

"Will this Worry Marble help you through the school assembly tomorrow?" I ask my brother, hoping he says the right thing.

"I think so?" says Mister. "I guess I feel a little less worried."

"You're looking at a very satisfied customer," I tell the crowd. "Now all you have to do is tell us your problems, and you

can have a Worry Marble by tomorrow.
Usually they cost two dollars, but you can
order one today for half price."

Amina and Charlie smile and nod.
They're in! Emmet looks around at all the
kids and seems surprised that so many
people are interested in my idea.

"I have a spelling test on Friday," says a second grader. "Do they help with spelling?"

Charlie is so nervous that he blurts out, "The color purple is associated with intelligence!"

"What about violin recitals?" asks another boy. "Mine is this weekend!"

"Orange boosts creativity!" Charlie tells him.

Charlie's facts are enough to convince the whole crowd. Suddenly, everyone is lining up to tell us their problems. Amina takes down their names and problems on a chart she's drawn up using my clipboard. There are dance recitals, dentist appointments and swim meets.

To top it off, every kindergartner ordered a red Worry Marble for tomorrow's assembly.

By the time recess is over, we have ninety-six names on our list. I don't like doing math, but I know that adds up to ninety-six dollars!

"I'm sure we'll get more orders at lunch," I tell my friends and Mister. "Then we'll split the profits between the four of us."

"Five of us," says Emmet. "After all, without me, you wouldn't have come up with the idea in the first place."

"Fine," I agree. "But if you want in, you have to help us with the business after school."

Emmet holds out his hand and we shake on it. "Deal."

CHAPTER 7
Let's Get Rolling

I was right about getting more orders. At lunch we got forty-two, and after the final bell we got another twelve. That's one hundred and fifty!

Charlie, Amina and I find Mister at our usual meeting spot after school. Emmet is late because he needs to give the other Emmas an excuse for why he's going to hang out with us. I don't really care what he tells them, but a small part of me wonders what Ruby will think about it.

Eventually, Emmet finds us, and we all walk over to my house. As we're about to go through the front door, I get a worried feeling in the pit of my stomach. My gut tells me that I might still be in trouble from this morning.

"There they are!" comes a familiar voice from inside. It's Nonna!

Mister rushes to the kitchen, and we all follow. Nonna is sitting at the table, drinking tea with Mom.

"Look at how big you are, Mister!" Nonna says as he hugs her. "It must be all that breakfast pizza you've been eating."

I feel better knowing Nonna could make a joke about this morning. Mom laughs and gets up to put out snacks. She's wearing a head-to-toe painting suit that used to be white, and has the hood on tight so that only her face is showing. She looks like an astronaut, and I cringe.

"Let me think here …" she says, surveying all the kids in the kitchen. "I know Charlie will want a slice of three cheese, and Amina likes it spicy with mushrooms." Then she turns to Emmet. "I don't think we've properly met."

I want to tell her he's an Emma and that's why he's never been over.

"I'm Emmet," he says quietly.

"Emmet, of course! I think your mom plays on an ultimate-frisbee team with my wife." Mom pulls out three Teresaria pizza boxes from the fridge and hands out plates.

"The team with pink shirts that have a pizza slice on the back?" asks Emmet politely.

"The Teresaria is the team sponsor," explains Mister with his mouth already full of food.

"Well, it's nice to meet you, Emmet," says my mom. "Help yourself to whatever slice you'd like." Mom turns to me and asks, "Pizza, Wednesday?"

"Don't we have anything else?" I ask. It's the kind of question that isn't a question, because I know that's all we ever have in the fridge.

"There's still some leftover breakfast pizza," she says, smiling.

"Three cheese it is!" I grab a slice and say thank you. I hope she knows it's the type of thank-you that's also an apology for this morning. She usually gets that kind of stuff.

When we're done, we clear our plates, and I tell Mom and Nonna that we're going to play hide-and-seek. Then I lead my friends upstairs to my room, where I explain the plan.

"My nonna can't know we're giving away the marbles," I tell them, "because they belonged to my nonno." I don't want to hurt Nonna's feelings, but a part of me thinks Nonno would have loved that his marbles were going to help people.

We make a game plan. I am "it" so I can run around the house pretending to look for people, but really, I'll be looking for marbles. Charlie, Amina and Mister each take an upstairs bedroom to search, and Emmet gets the bathroom. He's already proved himself useful in there earlier today.

Emmet lets us know he has to leave for tap class in an hour, so Amina sets the timer on her phone. I didn't know Emmet could tap dance. I tell him that's really cool.

"Everyone ready?" I ask. They all nod,

then scatter to their positions. "Ready or not, here I come!" I yell into the hall. Let the games begin!

I grab marbles from absolutely everywhere. Under couch cushions, in the junk drawer and even in the dirty laundry bin. When my pockets are heavy with marbles, I go back to my room to unload them on my bed, where there's already a growing pile. I'm about to go look for more, when I notice the calendar above my desk. There are big red circles around the words *FEED MOLLY'S CAT!* every day this week.

I leave a note on my bed for my friends, and just as I'm about to run out the front door, I find one more blue marble and shove it in my pocket.

I went to feed my neighbor's cat.
If I'm not back soon, send help!

—Wednesday

CHAPTER 8
Feline Not-So-Good

Molly is my tutor, and she lives three houses down from us. Whenever she goes away, I can get my allowance by feeding her cat, Harry. It's a strange name for a wrinkly, alien-looking cat that doesn't have any hair. I'm not even sure he's really a cat. But I am sure that Harry does *not* like me.

I bet you've heard of "scaredy cats," but Harry is the exact opposite. Harry isn't scared of anything. I think he can somehow climb walls, because he's always pouncing on me from above with his claws out. And he makes this awful crying sound, but when I get close to see if he's okay … SWAT! He scratches me. I'm beginning to wonder if this is worth the eight dollars I'm getting paid to feed him all week.

I unlock the door, sneak inside and walk as fast as I can to the kitchen. Molly has a whole side of the fridge just for Harry. She thinks he's human. I hold my breath and pour the rotten-foot-smelling dinner into his metal bowl. *Slooop!*

I quickly stand up and look around. Harry comes crashing down from on top of the fridge making horrible angry noises. He demolishes his food in seconds and then pounces on my shoelace. When I reach down to push him away, the blue marble falls out of my pocket and makes a loud *CLANK* as it falls into the metal bowl. Harry leaps toward his dish.

"HARRY! NO! BAD CAT!" I yell at him. But it's no use. He's already gulped down the marble.

"Oh nooo!" I say to the empty room.

Harry starts to moan. I know what happens whenever I try to help him, but I can't just leave him here like this. I grab a blanket from the couch and throw it over Harry. He's so surprised, he freezes, and I bundle him up in the blanket. Then I carry him out the door.

"You need to keep quiet," I whisper to Harry as we approach my house. I open the front door as slowly as I can and tiptoe up to my room without my mom or Nonna noticing.

Everyone is sitting on my bed counting marbles.

"One hundred and forty-nine," says Charlie. "We need one more to meet our goal."

They all look at me and then at the giant lump inside the blanket.

"What's that?" asks Emmet.

"It's Harry," I say as I place the cat on the bed.

"Not really, Wednesday," says Emmet. "It doesn't have any."

"Not *hairy*. His name is Harry," I tell them. "This is Molly's cat. And he ate one of my marbles a few minutes ago."

Harry groans, and the baggy skin around his throat wobbles.

"Is that why he looks like that?" asks Emmet, scrunching up his face.

"No, he's always this ugly," I tell him, "but he doesn't usually make this noise. I need to make sure he's going to be okay."

Amina picks up her phone and searches, *my cat just ate a marble will it die.*

"It says he will just poop it out," she tells us. "But you have to look out for lack of appetite and lethargy."

"I don't know what that means," I admit.

"It's when you're sleepy all the time," explains Charlie. "You need to tell your mom, Wednesday."

But before I can do anything else, Harry starts to make a terrible choking sound. Everyone jumps off the bed and stands around him.

"Do something, Wednesday!" cries Mister.

Harry wheezes louder, and then the marble shoots from his mouth right onto the bed. It's covered in slimy alien-cat sludge.

"One hundred and fifty!" says Mister.
"We did it!"

"Who gets that one?" asks Charlie.

"We'll save it for an Emma," says Amina,
laughing. Everyone looks at Emmet, but he's
laughing, too.

CHAPTER 9
They've Got the Power

I'm so relieved Harry is back to his old self but not at all happy that he's trying to rip apart my room. Once I finally catch him, I pass him to Emmet, the only person he hasn't tried to scratch.

We get back to business and start assigning a power for each marble color. But we don't get very far before the What-Ifs come up.

"What if it seems like we're taking advantage of people, since the marbles have no real powers?" asks Charlie.

"We're not!" I say right away.

Everyone is silent. They look at me with that are-you-sure look.

"The Worry Marble you gave me at recess did help me take my mind off tomorrow's assembly," says Mister.

"See!" I say. "And Amina, you said you wanted a business that helps people," I reply. "And that's what our Worry Marbles do, for the low price of a dollar."

"Plus, my pet rock cost five dollars, and it's just a rock," says Mister.

"Some of the worry stones on the internet are ten dollars!" says Amina after a quick search on her phone. "That makes me feel better about how much ours cost."

"Hmmm," I think aloud, "should we raise the price of our Worry Marbles?"

"NO!" everyone says at once.

Geez, it was just an idea.

We finish brainstorming the powers for each marble, and I write it all down on my clipboard.

MARBLE POWERS

red: courage

orange: creativity

yellow: happiness

blue: health

purple: intelligence

green: wealth

When it's time for Emmet to leave, he hands Harry to Charlie, who's not sure what to do with him. We all agree to meet across the street from school tomorrow morning to start selling.

Charlie, Amina, Mister and I spend the rest of the afternoon making tiny little name tags for the marbles, and when we're done, we put them all carefully into my backpack.

After I walk Charlie and Amina to the door and say goodbye, I'm surprised to see the Teresaria pulling into the driveway. Mum's never home this early.

"There was no dinner rush tonight," she says, getting out of the truck. "I thought we could all use a family picnic on the lawn instead!"

"Yay!" yells Mister, running down the front stairs. "Can I have a soda from the truck?"

"As long as no one spills it all over the pizza!" Mom calls after him. She gives my mum a quick kiss on the cheek and asks me to help Nonna outside.

In the kitchen, I steady Nonna as she gets up out of the chair. We walk slowly to the door together, arm in arm.

"Did you know your nonno had his own business?" she asks.

I do know, but I love hearing this story, so I pretend I don't remember. "What did he do again?" I ask.

"He had a deli," she starts. "That's where your mum first learned to make pizza. You remind me a lot of him, Wednesday."

"I do?" I ask. This is the first time she's ever said this, and it makes me proud. My nonno worked hard, and his business was really successful. His deli was even in a food magazine one time. My mum has the page framed on the wall of her food truck.

"You might think I've been too busy chatting with your mom to notice, but I've been watching you with your friends today. I have something for you." Nonna reaches into her pocket and pulls out a sparkly black marble. "You have to promise to keep this one. It was Nonno's favorite, so I think it will bring you luck in business, just like he had."

"I promise, Nonna," I say as I take the marble.

"And what a coincidence that it's called a *cat's*-eye marble." She winks at me and then looks up the stairs at my bedroom door. "You still have time to sneak him out the back door. Go on. I'll be fine on my own."

For once in my life, I'm at a loss for words. Harry isn't. A howl echoes through the house.

CHAPTER 10
Miss Moneybags

The next morning, I eat all my breakfast pizza with a smile. It makes my mom happy, plus it doesn't taste as bad when you eat it superfast.

Charlie rings the doorbell twice before my mom gets to the door. I walk downstairs slowly so the marbles don't rattle around in my backpack, but Mom still senses something's up.

"Are you going to tell me what's in your bag?" she asks.

"A new pursuit," I tell her.

"Are you a part of this new pursuit?" she asks Charlie.

Charlie shifts back and forth and starts turning red. "The word *backpack* was first used in the early nineteen hundreds. Before that, they were called moneybags!" he says. "And, um, yes, I'm a part of it."

"You learn something new every day," she says to Charlie. Then she turns to me and wishes us luck with "whatever we're up to." I make sure my nonno's black cat's-eye marble is in my pocket for extra luck, and we head to school with Mister.

We meet Amina right where we planned, just across the street from Harbor View Elementary. We're not allowed to sell things on school property, but no one said anything about selling things across the street.

"Where's Emmet?" asks Amina. People are starting to line up.

"Maybe he's just late?" I reply.

"Well, we can't wait for him," says Charlie. "We only have thirty minutes until the first bell, and we have a lot of customers to serve."

One by one, people hand Charlie their dollars. Then Mister and Amina hand out the marbles, and I cross the names off the list on my clipboard. When the first bell rings, we serve the last customer.

"We made a hundred and fifty dollars, just as planned," Charlie says as he finishes counting the money. "That's thirty dollars each, including Emmet. But where is he?"

There's no time to wonder about Emmet because we have to get to class before the second bell. I throw on my backpack, which now has all our money in it, and hold the straps tight.

When Charlie, Amina and I get to class, we see that Emmet is already sitting at his desk. And Emma M. is standing there whispering in his ear! She looks at me and laughs. I get a sinking feeling that they're making fun of me, and I feel stupid for thinking I could trust Emmet.

The second bell rings, and everyone takes their seats.

"Don't worry, Wednesday," Amina whispers to me. "It just means more money for us!"

I agree with Amina and send Emmet a look of disappointment. Sometimes my mom gives me that look, so I know how much it hurts.

For the first part of the morning, we have silent centers, which means we get to do a quiet activity. Amina chooses reading, and Charlie chooses his advanced math puzzles. I decide to hang out with Morten. I feel like he wants to play in his water tub today, but I can't find it anywhere. I go to the sink to look for it and find Emmet there, filling the tub. I guess he's decided to hang out with Morten, too.

Emmet finally speaks. "I did us a favor," he whispers.

"Letting us split the money between four people and not five?" I say coldly.

Emmet and I struggle to carry the tub full of water back to Morten's tank. It doesn't help that I'm wearing my backpack everywhere I go.

"If you didn't notice, not one Emma showed up to ruin anything this morning," he says as we set the tub down beside the tank.

He's right. I didn't see an Emma. Or Ruby.

"I made sure to keep them away because I know they like to get in the way of your plans," he explains.

I sign out Morten and lift him into the water tub. I can tell he's excited to soak, because I know him really well. Once Morten is in the tub, Emmet gently pours water from a cup onto his back.

"So, this morning when you were whispering with Emma M., it wasn't about me?" I ask Emmet as I sit on the floor beside Morten.

"Well, not exactly," explains Emmet. "Yesterday, when Dakota came to get you in class, Emma M. did send me to spy on you in the bathroom, but —"

"I knew that's what that double wink was about!" I say a little too loudly. People turn and shush me. "I had a feeling you were faking being nice," I whisper.

"No!" Emmet protests. "At first, I was spying, but then I realized Mister could use my help. And I wanted to help him, honestly. The family tree project isn't easy for everyone."

"I get that," I say.

Emmet continues. "And then it was fun to be part of it all. Like, not being told what to do, and eating pizza and holding that weird creature from your neighbor's house."

"Harry."

"Yeah," Emmet says. "So this morning, when I saw you guys setting up across the street, I told Emma M. that the other Emmas were looking for her on the playground."

"Were they?" I ask.

"They're always looking for one another." He smiles. "It was one of your half-truths. I also told Emma M. just now how much fun I had hanging out with you, which is why she was laughing."

Morten splashes around in the water. I think I hear him sigh with happiness, if lizards can even sigh.

For the rest of silent centers, I tell Emmet about how we sold all the Worry Marbles. He seems pretty impressed. We figure we can take more orders at recess and hopefully sell the same amount tomorrow.

Ms. Gelson gives us the five-minute warning, and the class starts tidying up. We put Morten back in his tank along with some dried crickets, his favorite treat. Then we wash our hands and take our seats.

Math comes next, but the only math I'm interested in is calculating the cost* of getting more customers to buy our Worry Marbles.

*This calculation has a long, boring name: customer acquisition cost. Basically it's the money you spend to tell people about your product, divided by the number of new customers. This tells you how much each customer cost you, but if you keep them happy, it's a one-time fee!

CHAPTER 11

Extra Toppings

Recess doesn't go the way I thought. We try to take more orders, but people want to see if the Worry Marbles work at the assembly before buying them. I'm suddenly nervous because the fate of our business is out of my hands.

When we get back to class, we line up to go to the assembly. Ms. Gelson lets me know it's fine to leave my backpack in the cubby area if I want. But when she sees me hesitate, she says, "It's okay to keep a backpack close for creature comfort!"

Inside the gym, I sit on the floor next to Charlie and Amina, and then Emmet slips in next to me. A voice comes from behind us.

"This is your last chance, Emmet," says Emma M. "It's them or us."

"It doesn't have to be like that," Emmet replies. He tries to say more, but Emma M. interrupts.

"Whatever, Emmet," she says. "Have fun playing with marbles all day."

The lights dim as two sixth graders walk to the microphone to start the assembly. Everyone goes quiet as they recite the land acknowledgment. Then they remind us that today is the first of many assemblies for Poet-Tree Month, and they invite the kindergarten class to come up and read their poem.

I hold my breath. This is it.

One by one, each kindergartner holds up their family tree and adds a part about their family to the poem. And one by one, each student does it perfectly.

Mister goes last. In a very confident voice, he says:

"My family is like a pizza slice.
We can be sweet and spicy,
and not always nice.
But we stick together in the pan,
And help each other whenever we can."

Mister holds up his family tree, which he must have redone last night. Instead of a tree, it's a pizza slice with our family as toppings.

The applause is unlike anything I've ever heard. I look around and see dollar signs everywhere.

Mister hands the microphone to Principal Webb.

"Thank you, kindergartners! What a fantastic poem, and read so delightfully!" she says.

Everyone claps again, and many of Mister's classmates hold out their Worry Marbles to show me they worked. It couldn't be better advertising.

Principal Webb looks at all the marbles and then at me. As the class walks back to their spot, she taps one of the students on the shoulder and asks her a question. The girl shows her marble to the principal and says a few words I can't make out.

The rest of the assembly is pretty normal. There's an announcement about the senior girls' basketball team winning again and a reminder about the upcoming long weekend. I'm sure there's more, but I zone out when I start to think about everyone in the gym being a potential customer.

"Thank you, everyone, for joining us today," says Principal Webb. "I'd like to leave you with one final thought before we go. Our school is just like the family trees so beautifully created by our kindergarten class. Each class is a branch. You are the leaves. Today, you might think about what it means to be connected to one another in this way."

We all nod our heads, but I can't shake the feeling Principal Webb is speaking directly to me and my friends.

"Do you think that if the leaf beside you needed something to help it grow, you should help it and not expect anything in return?" Now I swear she's looking at us.

Charlie, Amina and Emmet look at the floor.

Principal Webb dismisses each class one by one, until just Mister's class and my class are left. She calls over Ms. Gelson and Mister's teacher, Mrs. Yao, and they stand in a tight circle discussing something that seems important.

I try to read their lips to make out what they're talking about, and I'm certain I see Principal Webb say my name.

CHAPTER 12
Logging Off

When we're finally allowed to leave the gym, we head straight to the computer lab. We can do what we want for an hour in computer class, as long as we're typing and looking at the monitor. Charlie starts a group chat with me and Amina, and I invite Emmet to join.

Charlie
I think we should give back the money.

Amina
I agree with Charlie. I don't want Principal Webb to call my parents.

Charlie
We could give it back at lunch, before we have a chance to get in trouble.

Emmet
I think so, too. Sorry, Wednesday.

I log off from the chat and don't make eye contact with my friends. The thought of giving back all the money makes me angry. After all, we sold a real product that actually helped people.

I look up facts about marbles to research our business idea and to avoid my friends. I find a website that tells me marbles were used by kids in ancient Egypt. I really badly want to tell Charlie this fact, and Amina, too, because she's been to Egypt and even saw a pyramid in real life. I also want to tell Emmet about another fact I read on the website, that rare marbles can sell for thousands of dollars. He likes the idea of making money as much as I do.

But I can't tell them right now because a feeling is starting to creep in that maybe my friends are right, and I'm not ready yet to be wrong. I liked helping the kindergartners, and not just because we made money. Does giving back the money mean admitting that helping them was a bad idea? I pull Nonno's shiny black marble out of my pocket. It's supposed to help with my business, but all it does is make me feel like I failed at being an entrepreneur.

I decide I need a change of scenery and ask if I can go get a drink from the water fountain. I bring Althea as my buddy.

Althea takes a drink from the fountain after me, and I wander over to Ms. Eleanor, our librarian, who's busy placing art in the display case near the library's entrance. At our school, if your art makes it into the display case, it's a big deal. One of the pieces is Mister's family pizza. He is a giant piece of pepperoni right in the middle, and I'm a spicy hot pepper next to him.

"Your brother is one lucky guy!" Ms. Eleanor tells me.

"Yes, he's going to be really excited when he sees it on display," I reply.

"He is," she agrees, "but that's not what I meant. He's lucky to have someone like you who will always be by his side."

"I did help Mister with the assembly," I explain, "but I didn't do it alone."

Something my nonno once told me flashes into my mind: *Don't surround yourself with smart people unless you want to learn from them.* I thank Ms. Eleanor and head back to the computers.

It's time to listen to my friends.

I log back into the chat and let everyone know I agree that we should give the money back at lunch, but that doesn't mean we didn't make a difference.

After computer class, it's lunchtime. I meet everyone in the lunchroom and slip into the empty seat beside Charlie. Word travels fast that we're closing shop. People form a long line in front of us, and I open my backpack.

"Goodbye, money," I say as I hand it all over to Charlie.

"We can make it all back next time, Wednesday," Charlie assures me.

The first person in line is Mister. He didn't even buy his marble, so I don't know why he lined up.

"I just want you to know that the Worry Marble worked," he says. "I wasn't nervous at all during the assembly."

"Mine worked, too!" says another kid in line.

"Me, too," someone else pipes up.

My product actually did help people, just like I thought! It makes me realize that being an entrepreneur means there's going to be ups and downs. Sometimes, your product will work, but your business still won't take off. But the important thing is to keep trying.

"Everyone, listen up!" I say to the kids in the line. "We'll refund your money if you give back the marbles, but I hope you'll remember that the Worry Marbles really did work. So next time we have something to sell, trust us and come back as valuable customers."

Everyone, including my friends, is very happy with what I just said, and we all high-five each other. Everything seems to be going great until an announcement comes over the PA system: "Will Wednesday Wilson and Emmet Easton please come directly to the office."

CHAPTER 13

Sweetening the Deal

"I've never been to the office," Emmet admits when we are just about to go in.

"Let me do the talking," I tell him.

We walk into the office to see Principal Webb, Ms. Gelson and Mrs. Yao smiling at us. It catches me off guard.

"Wednesday, Emmet, come on in," says Principal Webb, motioning us into her office. We sit down. I still can't tell if we're in trouble, but I'm never a good judge of that. I look at Emmet, who's shaking he's so nervous.

Principal Webb begins talking. "Mrs. Yao has brought to my attention a matter involving the kindergartners."

This can't be good, I think.

"Apparently you two saved the day," Principal Webb tells us.

"We *what*?" I say.

"Yes!" says Mrs. Yao. "Wednesday, you saved the assembly by sharing your special marbles with my kindergarten class. And Emmet, Mister told me that you're the one who gave him the idea to really think outside the box for his family tree. I wanted to thank you personally. I've decided to change the family tree project for next year so that it invites all kinds of creative interpretations."

I can hardly believe what I'm hearing. I look over at Emmet, who's also now realizing we aren't here to get in trouble.

"As a reward," says Ms. Gelson, "I'm going to add a jelly bean to the jar for each kindergartner you helped — which means a jelly bean party this afternoon."

A jelly bean party? My mouth starts to water.

Ms. Gelson and Mrs. Yao head back to class, but Principal Webb asks Emmet and me to stay for another minute.

"I'm happy to hear you made such a positive impact on your school community," she starts. "*Giving back* is so valuable. *Worth* far more than you think. Don't you agree?"

"We do," I tell Principal Webb. "And don't worry, we've been doing a ton of giving back lately."

"On that note," she says, "the strangest thing happened yesterday. I found a marble and put it in the bowl on my desk, and then it disappeared. Wednesday, I thought you might know what happened to it, since you seem to be quite the marble collector."

I try to look surprised and shake my head.

"Did it have a rainbow center?" asks Emmet quickly.

"Yes," Principal Webb answers. "It did!"

"Like the one under your desk?" Emmet crawls under the desk and picks up a rainbow marble.

He hands it to Principal Webb. "It must have somehow fallen on the ground when you weren't looking."

Principal Webb looks back and forth between us with suspicion, but there's nothing she can say besides thank you. She takes the marble back and dismisses us.

On the way to class, I look at Emmet in disbelief. "How did you do that?"

"When Mister high-fived me at lunch, the marble ended up in my hand. I meant to give it back to him, but then we were called to the office," explains Emmet. "When I crawled under the desk, I just fished it out of my pocket."

"So it was a lucky marble, after all!" I say.

"I'm sorry I had to give it back to Principal Webb," says Emmet.

I put my hand in my pocket and rub Nonno's black cat's-eye marble, happy I still have it.

"That's okay. I have another lucky marble now that I'll be more careful with," I explain. "Let's hurry back! We have a jelly bean party we don't want to be late for."

THE END

EPILOGUE*

The jelly bean party was as awesome as it sounds. But eating a handful of jelly beans wasn't even the best part! After the class finished the whole jar, we still had time to spare before the end of the day. So we brainstormed all the things we could do with the glass jar now that it was empty.

And guess whose idea won. Mine! I suggested we fill the jar with Worry Marbles so that anyone could borrow

*A fancy word for the REAL end

one when they need extra help. Then once the marble has helped them, they could put it back so there are always lots of marbles in the jar to go around. I offered up my nonno's collection to fill the jar, and I am sure my nonna would think this is the best possible use of his marbles. Everyone in the class agreed it was a good idea. And even though the Emmas rolled their eyes, I could tell they actually kind of liked it, too.

I bet you want to know what happened with Emmet and me, right? It's finally safe to say we're friends now. There's no way he's reporting back to the Emmas, because then he'd be spying on himself, which isn't even a thing. At the end of class, I heard him telling Ruby all about scary Harry. He was making choking noises and pretending a marble popped out of his mouth into his hand. She laughed really hard. I wonder if she remembers how when Harry was a kitten, we used to think he was a giant rat.

I wonder a lot of things about Ruby lately, and for some reason I feel like my next business will have something to do with her.

Acknowledgments*

Wednesday and Mister could not have come to life without the voices of my own children, Dario and Oakland, who are of mixed race (Black, Cherokee and white) and opened my eyes to the lack of representation in books for children. They spent countless hours adding their own voices to my manuscript to provide authenticity to my characters where I, as a white woman, fell short. I hope this story resonates with other kids and shows that everyone deserves to have themselves reflected in a book, no matter what.

*A fancy word for saying thank you

I am eternally thankful to my editor, Katie Scott at Kids Can Press, for treating Wednesday as though she were a real person and getting to know her in a way I never imagined possible. Katie is one of the main reasons Wednesday is as multidimensional as every reader who picks up this book. She held me accountable throughout the writing of the manuscript to ensure we weren't perpetuating any stereotypes or tropes, and had the hard conversations when they mattered most.

A massive thank-you to Morgan Goble, illustrator extraordinaire, who took on this project and captured all the characters so wonderfully. Morgan's immeasurable talent is what brought this series to life. My kids will forever be reflected in these pages, something we only dreamed possible when we started this project years ago.

Thank you to my agent, Claire Anderson-Wheeler, at Regal Hoffmann, for believing in both me and Wednesday right away. And finally, there are so many moving parts behind the scenes in a series like Wednesday Wilson, and the team at Kids Can Press is second to none. It takes far more than an author to make a book, and I hope they all share in this achievement alongside me.

Bree Galbraith is a writer and graphic designer who lives with her family in Vancouver, British Columbia. Her critically acclaimed picture books include *Nye, Sand and Stones, Usha and the Stolen Sun* and *Milo and Georgie*. Bree holds a Masters in Creative Writing from the University of British Columbia. Visit breegalbraith.com to learn more.

Morgan Goble has been drawing since she could first hold a crayon. A graduate of the Bachelor of Illustration program at Sheridan College, Morgan is also the illustrator of *Wednesday Wilson Gets Down to Business*. She lives with her husband and their cat, Noni, in London, Ontario. To learn more about Morgan, visit morgangoble.ca.

LOOKING FOR MORE OF THE INDOMITABLE*
WEDNESDAY WILSON?

MORE ADVENTURES TO COME!

*This means impossible to defeat